ERIC CARLE
The Greedy Python

by Richard Buckley   illustrated by Eric Carle

READY-TO-READ

SIMON SPOTLIGHT

New York   London   Toronto   Sydney   New Delhi

SIMON SPOTLIGHT

An imprint of Simon & Schuster Children's Publishing Division
1230 Avenue of the Americas, New York, New York 10020
Text copyright © 1985, 2012 by Richard Buckley
Illustrations copyright © 1985 by Eric Carle
Originally published in the United States by Picture Book Studio 1985
First Simon Spotlight Ready-to-Read edition 2012
For information about special discounts for bulk purchases, please contact Simon & Schuster Special Sales at 1-866-506-1949 or
business@simonandschuster.com.
The Simon & Schuster Speakers Bureau can bring authors to your live event. For more information or to book an event contact
the Simon & Schuster Speakers Bureau at 1-866-248-3049 or visit our website at www.simonspeakers.com.
Manufactured in the United States of America 0616 LAK
6 8 10 9 7 5
Library of Congress Cataloging-in-Publication Data
Buckley, Richard, 1938-
The greedy python / by Richard Buckley ; illustrated by Eric Carle. — 1st ed.
p. cm. — (Ready-to-read)
Summary: A greedy python eats to excess, finally eating himself.
ISBN 978-1-4424-4576-5 (pbk.) — ISBN 978-1-4424-4577-2 (hardcover)
[1. Stories in rhyme. 2. Greed—Fiction. 3. Pythons—Fiction. 4. Snakes—Fiction. 5. Food habits—Fiction.] I. Carle, Eric, ill. II. Title.
PZ8.3.B8474Gr 2012
[E]—dc23
2011025822
This book was previously published with slightly different text.

Half hidden
in the jungle green,
the biggest snake
that there has been
looped back and forth
and in between.

The giant snake was

very strong,

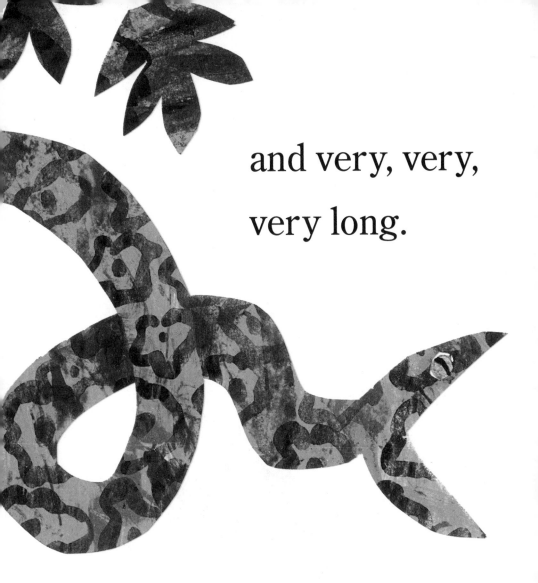

and very, very,
very long.

He had a big, huge appetite.
His belly stretched
from left to right.

He quickly gobbled
in one bite
all animals
that came in sight:

a mouse that hurried
to and fro,

a frog that jumped up
from below,

a bat that hung
from his left toe,

a fish that swam
a bit too slow,

a bird that flew a bit too low,

a porcupine

still half asleep,

a monkey who was
in mid-leap,

a leopard sitting in a tree,

a buffalo who came to see.

An elephant,
complete with trunk,
was swallowed
in a single chunk.
"I am too big
for you!"
he cried.

"No, you are not!"
the snake replied.

At last the python's meal

was done,

and he lay resting

in the sun.

The animals inside of him
began to jump and fly
and swim.

And when they all
began to kick,
the snake began
to feel quite sick.

He coughed the whole lot
up again.
Each one of them, and there
were ten.

He soon felt better.
What is more,
he was hungrier than before.
He had not learned
a single thing.

His greed was quite
astonishing.

He saw his own tail,
long and curved,
and thought that lunch
was being served.

He closed his jaws

on his own rear,

then swallowed hard . . .

. . . and disappeared!